This book belongs to:

....

HOTHOUSE

Published in 2017
by Igloo Books Ltd
Cottage Farm
Sywell
NN6 0BJ
www.igloobooks.com

FIR003 0917
2 4 6 8 10 9 7 5 3
ISBN 978-1-78670-168-8

Written by Melanie Joyce
Illustrated by Helen Rowe

Printed and manufactured in China

The Wheels
on the Bus

The wheels on the bus go round and round,
round and round, round and round.
The wheels on the bus go round and round, all day long.

The animals on the bus get on and off, on and off, on and off.
The animals on the bus get on and off, all day long.

The money on the bus goes jingle, jangle, jingle,
jingle, jangle, jingle, jingle, jangle, jingle.
The money on the bus goes jingle, jangle, jingle, all day long.

The driver on the bus goes, "Move on back,
move on back, move on back."
The driver on the bus goes, "Move on back," all day long.

The bell on the bus goes ding, ding, ding,
ding, ding, ding, ding, ding, ding.
The bell on the bus goes ding, ding, ding, all day long.

The monkeys on the bus go, "Oo-oo-oo, oo-oo-oo, oo-oo-oo."
The monkeys on the bus go, "Oo-oo-oo," all day long.

The engine on the bus goes vroom, vroom, vroom,
vroom, vroom, vroom, vroom, vroom, vroom.
The engine on the bus goes vroom, vroom, vroom, all day long.

The horn on the bus goes beep, beep, beep,
beep, beep, beep, beep, beep, beep.
The horn on the bus goes beep, beep, beep, all day long.

The mommy hippos go chatter, chatter, chatter, chatter, chatter, chatter, chatter, chatter, chatter. The mommy hippos go chatter, chatter, chatter, all day long.

The daddy elephants go nod, nod, nod, nod, nod, nod, nod, nod, nod.
The daddy elephants go nod, nod, nod, all day long.

The wipers on the bus go swish, swish, swish,
swish, swish, swish, swish, swish, swish.
The wipers on the bus go swish, swish, swish, all day long.

The puddles on the road go splash, splash, splash,
splash, splash, splash, splash, splash, splash.
The puddles on the road go splash, splash, splash, all day long.

The baby lion cubs go, "Wah, wah, wah, wah, wah, wah, wah, wah, wah."
The baby lion cubs go, "Wah, wah, wah," all day long.

The little tiger tots go giggle, giggle, giggle,
giggle, giggle, giggle, giggle, giggle, giggle.
The little tiger tots go giggle, giggle, giggle, all day long.

The stop lights outside go stop, wait, go,
stop, wait, go, stop, wait, go.
The stop lights outside go stop, wait, go, all day long.

The signals on the bus go blink, blink, blink,
blink, blink, blink, blink, blink, blink.
The signals on the bus go blink, blink, blink, all day long.

A B C

The grandpa gorillas go snore, snore, snore,
snore, snore, snore, snore, snore, snore.
The grandpa gorillas go snore, snore, snore, all day long.

The grandma crocodiles go, "Shh, shh, shh,
shh, shh, shh, shh, shh, shh."
The grandma crocodiles go, "Shh, shh, shh," all day long.

The bus goes round the town until the sun goes down,
the sun goes down, the sun goes down.
The bus goes round the town until the sun goes down, all day long.

The animals on the bus go, "Here's my stop!
Here's my stop! Here's my stop!"
The animals on the bus go, "Here's my stop!" all day long.